Dancer, Dreamer, Seer

LIANA BROOKS

OTHER WORKS

ALL I WANT FOR CHRISTMAS

All I Want For Christmas Is A Reaper
All I Want For Christmas Is A Werewolf

FLEET OF MALIK

Bodies In Motion
Change of Momentum

HEROES AND VILLAINS

Even Villains Fall In Love
Even Villains Go To The Movies
Even Villains Have Interns
Even Villains Play The Hero (books 1 – 3 omnibus)
The Polar Terror

TIME AND SHADOWS

The Day Before
Convergence Point
Decoherence

SHORTER WORKS

Fey Lights
Prime Sensations
Darkness and Good

Find other works by the author at
www.lianabrooks.com

Dancer, Dreamer, Seer

INKLET #83

LIANA BROOKS

Inkprint PRESS
www.inkprintpress.com

Print ISBN: 978-1-922434-23-4
eBook ISBN: 9798201832025

www.inkprintpress.com

National Library of Australia Cataloguing-in-Publication Data
Brooks, Liana 1982 –
Dancer, Dreamer, Seer
60 p.
ISBN: 978-1-922434-23-4
Inkprint Press, Canberra, Australia
1. Fiction—Fantasy—Epic 2. Fiction—Fantasy—Historical 3. Fiction—Short Stories

First Print Edition: June 2022
Cover image © Mark Frost via Pixabay
Cover design © Inkprint Press
Interior art © Amy Laurens

DANCER, DREAMER, SEER

"I'M NEVER GOING TO GET THIS RIGHT," Dallon told his twin Dasha without looking up.

"Arch your foot a little more," she advised while she picked at some stitching. Dallon tried, but failed to catch the knife with his foot. "Perhaps there's another dance you're better at?" she asked.

Dallon nodded and began another dance, a series of fluid, violent motion. A series of motion that turned Dallon from a twelve-year-old boy into a frightening predator, a fierce protector, and a man.

After several minutes, he stopped. "I do that one best."

"Which one is it?" Dasha said, unaffected.

Dance was magic, each movement, each step a call to the inner-being, the holder of the magic.

Every child learned Dance, and as the last years of youth faded and adulthood beckoned, mothers and fathers pulled their youngsters in to teach them the secrets of Dance.

Dance of Courtship. Dance of the Maiden, Dance of the Lady, Dance of Men, and all the Dances needed to work the magic of each individual calling.

Everyone from the baker to the Lord of the Land had a Dance. Dallon was trying hard to find the one that suited him best so he could Dance for his apprenticeship.

"Dance of the Lord," Dallon smiled happily. "I thought it would make Father proud."

Dasha nodded. "Mother would prefer you to be a warrior, or a scholar perhaps. She does favor the scholars when they ask for dinner."

"Mother favors anyone who knocks and begs supper. I've never seen her turn anyone away."

"She will one day."

Dallon didn't need to ask what Dasha meant; there wasn't a need to. The women of their blood had always been gifted with vision, the ability sometimes as small as knowing the right path to choose, and sometimes as frightening as Dasha's ability to know the future, without truly knowing it.

"So, which Dance shall I do?" Dallon continued as if his sister-twin had not spoken.

Dallon was seven months younger, which by law made them twins, and by math made them a confusion. No one had ever commented on the impossibility—unless Dallon was born *very* early—but occasionally the twins had thought about it separately.

"You do know I'm not supposed to see these Dances?" Dasha questioned, putting aside her stitch work. They were sitting along the side of the manor house, Dallon Dancing in the dirt, and Dasha sitting on the stoop in the shade. "Mother was quite insistent that some things are best left to mystery. Especially the Dance of Men." She looked at her brother shrewdly.

He shook his head. "I'm not showing you that one."

"Why not?" she asked indignantly. "You'll watch me at the Courtship Dance on the new moon, why can't I see your Dance?"

"Because you'll laugh." Dallon joined her on the stoop. "Father explained it quite well actually. He said only your intended lady can be lured by the magic, others will laugh. So I won't show you, because you'll laugh. But if you're a very good sister I shall show your husband Father's moves, if I like him."

Dasha snorted. "Men! You and your silly secrets." She picked at her stitching again. "I like the Warrior Dance best," she said distractedly.

"Yes." Dallon tossed his head to get hair out of his eyes. "That's the hardest, so of course you'd like it."

"It looks easy enough," she said.

"Right." He stood and began walking slowly through the Lord's Dance. "I like this Dance, it's almost like the Dance of Men."

Dasha frowned. "Why is that?"

"Because it binds a Lord to the land the same way the Dance of Men binds a man to his wife. It connects them, splits and twines their souls. When I do the steps I can feel the whole land around me. Do you know how a tree feels on a bright day?"

She shook her head.

"It feels marvelous! And the fresh plowed fields? There's joy, and in winter there is quiet peace, and in spring everything feels like it's about to stand and Dance."

"I hope they make you a Lord, otherwise we'll never hear the end of it." Dasha smiled. "You really would make a terrible warrior. I wonder what warriors feel?"

"Cold maybe?" Dallon guessed, speeding his footwork and improvising to the tune only he could hear. "What do you need to feel to kill? Maybe the Dance takes away your feelings, takes the fear and hides it so you can defend the land."

Dasha shuddered. "I just had a horrible thought, what if a woman were bound to a warrior? Imagine what the poor girl would feel? It would be an absolute terror!"

Dallon stopped. "That was wicked of you," he said, meeting his twins' eye.

"It's true," she said. "Imagine a woman bound to such a man; a mother with no feeling?"

"Or a bear betwixt cub and hunter."

"A mother gone cold?"

"A woman defending her lover's heart? A woman breathing two breaths to keep her husband alive while he fights, a woman taking the pain so her love can return to her?"

"You make it sound romantic and noble," Dasha grumbled.

"Grandfather was a warrior," Dallon reminded her as he returned to his footwork.

Dasha watched quietly until he finished. "I still like the Warrior's Dance best."

"Try it then." Dallon gestured to the flattened ground. "Water," he whispered with closed eyes. A small fountain appeared a moment before being sucked back into the summer-dry ground.

"You shouldn't do that," Dasha chided. "If you want water run along to the kitchen and fetch us both some. I'm going to try the Dance."

Dallon snorted, but ran off. When he returned with two cold mugs of berry juice, Dasha was performing the Warrior's Dance, fast, and flawless.

His jaw dropped. He dropped too, down onto the stoop to watch.

She finished with an added flourish that made her glow against even the midday sun. His sister looked dangerous and distant.

"What do you feel?" he whispered.

"I feel the sun very bright, and I can hear all the animals' breath, and the heartbeat of every human. I know the thoughts of people, if I try. But I feel... bereft." She frowned and dropped the pose. "How odd, it feels as if something is missing. I can't name it, but there is definitely something not right."

"Maybe it's cause you're a girl." Dallon offered her some juice.

She sipped thoughtfully and then shook her head.

"Do you want to kill people?" he asked.

"No, but I know where everything is. I could walk down the street and know who our enemies are."

"You could do that anyway, you can see it!" Dallon said.

"This feels different. It's knowledge without knowing, you know?" It was Dallon's turn to shake his head. "I know things, but only if I don't think about it. When I think about it, the knowing goes away."

"Well, it can't be the same for men." Dallon hadn't been able to get the steps of the Warrior's Dance, especially the tricky part where you had to pull weapons from the ground with your toes. Speaking of… "Where did you get the knives? They better not be Cook's or he'll be cross."

"These?" Dasha frowned down at the three throwing blades in her hand. "I thought you left them, they were there when I needed them in the Dance."

Dallon picked up one of the blades and examined it closely. "It looks real, but I have wooden ones to practice with. Do they feel like anything to you?"

Dasha stood and pulled her power to her, tugging on the inner-being and focusing its energy on the weapons. "They feel new, just born, but they will see blood. Blood of hate, blood of love, blood to bind, blood to kill." Dasha dropped the knives. "What confusing little weapons." She cursed, kicking them aside. "They don't know anything except blood, no faces and no names, no feeling but blood. Hot and violent." She looked to her brother for guidance.

"While you're with Mama for lessons I'll take them to the peddler. Let them travel before they find blood," Dallon advised.

Dasha nodded and kicked the knives toward her brother lightly.

They finished their juice in silence, each lost in their own thoughts.

"Dasha?" Mama's voice rang through the airy hall behind them.

Dasha responded silently on a feminine mind thread. "I ought to go." She stood and collected her things. Pausing at the edge of the door, she turned. "Dallon?"

"Hmm?"

"What kind of binding requires blood?" she asked quietly, almost fearfully.

"None," he answered curtly. He stood and picked up the knives. "No binding of good requires blood."

Dasha nodded. "Sell them quickly."

Her twin agreed.

"We have a problem!" Dallon announced two months later as he arrived like a small whirlwind in Dasha's private courtyard. The small garden surrounded by high trellises and filled to overflowing with fragrant—and thorny—flowers had been planted for Dasha at her birth and tended in turn by every female relative that had paid call. It was Dasha's private sanctuary, a place to retreat when the heartbeat of the future grew to loud. She had started coming here with her mother before she could walk, and she had begun tending the flowers before she could say their names.

Only Dallon entered here besides her now.

Dasha set down her assigned stitch work for the day and studied her flustered brother. "What is the problem exactly?" It had been a long day; one spent avoiding people and their prying eyes. One of the maids was about to have a babe and she wanted desperately to plague Dasha about the child's future. Dasha knew the girl desperately needed not to know.

"I can't do the Lord's Dance." Dallon sighed and sat in the center of the garden with a huff, totally ignoring the chair set out by the table under the canopy where Dasha was.

She rolled her eyes. "Your legs seem to be just fine."

"My legs are not the problem," he said. "The problem is that every Lord must have another course of study, which means I need to know another Dance!"

"Since when?" Dasha frowned.

"Since forever I guess, but Father didn't know that was the Dance I had picked, so he didn't tell me." Dallon picked at the grass without pulling it. He looked ready to cry.

"Well then, we'll just have to do the obvious." Dasha smiled and settled back to her task of embroidering presentation clothes for the maid's babe.

Dallon looked up warily. "What, exactly, is obvious to 'we'?"

"We trade places."

"We what?"

"Has your hearing gone bad?" Dasha lifted an eyebrow. "It's simple really, I'll Dance the Warrior's Dance for you, and you can be trained as a Warrior."

Dallon gaped at her. "Are you moon mad or is this your idea of a joke?"

"I'm neither." She smiled back at her embroidery. "It seems to be the simplest solution to me."

"Except we'll be caught as soon as you Dance!"

She shrugged. "I'll cut my hair. Your Dance isn't until after the Courtship Dance, I can find an excuse to cut my hair like yours. Lice maybe, or a cooking fire?" Dasha sounded so calm as she talked about infesting herself with plagues and burning herself alive.

Girls, Dallon decided, were not worth half the trouble. "And what happens when I go to class and have no talent? You Dance so well they'll expect the same from me!"

"Practice will make up for natural inability, and even better, you can come share the lessons with me." Dasha positively beamed.

Dallon shook his head. "You have your own lessons!"

"I have Lady Lessons from Mamma, that isn't the same as your tutelage. It certainly isn't exerting. I'll spend hours going over household accounts and reviewing the staff and visiting crofters. And when that is over I'll be sent to my garden to be calm, practice the Dance of the Maiden, and stitch whatever abomination Mother has devised for me today." She looked with distaste at the piece she was working on. "The least you could do as my twin is rescue me a few hours a day by sharing what you're learning."

"I can't!" Dallon protested.

His sister's eyes sparkled. "You will."

"Really?"

She nodded.

"Is it for the best?"

She paused and cocked her head to the side as if listening. "For the best?

Yes, this is the best choice," she answered in a tone Dallon knew meant she was giving only part of an answer.

"Is it for the *good*?"

Dasha nodded.

"Will it make the family happy?"

Dasha frowned. "For a time, and then not, and then yes," she answered cryptically.

"What?" Dallon demanded.

"What?" she echoed.

"What do you *mean*?"

"What do I mean by what?" She looked confused. "What did I say?"

"You said something about this making us happy, then not, then yes. What is that supposed to mean?" He stood and strode toward his twin.

"I have no idea. I have trouble focusing on my future you know. I suspect it means that this is the best." Dasha resumed stitching.

Dallon watched her quietly. He sat and ate the food she had brought for him. Dasha always knew when he was coming. Undoubtedly she had thought long and hard about their options before he even knew they needed them.

"*Can* you see your future?" Dallon asked.

Dasha shook her head. "I see bits and pieces, I know a few things. I knew I was going to break my arm that one time we climbed on the roof. And I know sometime I'll be hurt, and I'll hurt someone I care for, but I don't know how." She fell quiet as if she were debating admitting more. "I know that I won't marry in the village. And I won't marry soon," she whispered. A tear rolled down her cheek. "I'll be the last of my year to marry."

"Dasha!" Dallon exclaimed in horror and went to hug his sister. "Don't cry, don't cry. Why are you crying?" He looked for a bee sting.

"No one wants me!" she wailed softly. "I'm not pretty, I can't Dance!"

"Oh, hush-a-bye sweet one," Dallon whispered as their Mother did when Dasha woke with the night terrors of Dreamers. "Hush now, you're loved. Mamma loves you, Poppa loves you, I love you. So what if the silly village boys don't see. Most girls don't marry until their fourth or fifth Dance. Don't worry now." Dallon reached for the inner-being; he was twin-born even if he wasn't a born twin. With effort, he could access his sister's talent. It hurt and left him weaker than he cared to admit after watching her do it so easily, but for this he was willing to sacrifice and take on the headache.

He clumsily touched the inner-being, falling awkwardly into the place of Knowing. "He loves you more than words, and binds you closer than love. He holds you higher than self, and pulls you back from the brink." Dallon frowned at his own voice; it sounded strange, too old, and too sad. He could feel the land in the place of Knowing and it wasn't happy. He could feel his sister and she felt strange, twisted, ravaged, powerful. "You are walking a very dangerous edge."

"Go further," Dasha whispered through her tears.

Dallon focused again and pushed further. He'd never gone more than a few years ahead, but now…

Slowly he crept along, beaten by the winds of emotion and knowledge in such a place as this. Then he touched what she had seen, the outcome of his twisted, ravaged, powerful sister; peace was on the other side. "Is it necessary?"

"I can't find another way there," she whispered. She looked up, brown eyes pleading. "I'm scared. Seers aren't supposed to feel like that. Dreamers should never feel like that. And that's what I am!" She started weeping again. "I hate me!"

"Shush, hush now, don't worry," Dallon wrapped his arms around her. "You won't be alone. You're bound." She shook her head into his shoulder. "Yes you are, hear me, you are bound."

"Twin born aren't bound," Dasha shot back.

"But you're bound to your other aren't you?" Dallon was guessing, he wasn't very good at interpreting all the things he learned in the place of Knowing. It was hard enough to find bits to translate; it was even harder to remember. In a few hours all he would have is a headache, and quite possibly a heartache.

Dasha bit her lip and shrugged with a weak nod. "I can't tell. I hate me! Why can't I tell? Why would I do that to everyone? Why would I be like that? Did you feel me?"

Dallon nodded solemnly, the wisdom of twelve years as the Seer's twin shining in his eyes. "You are bound. I don't know how, but you are. And you will be bound further when he finds you. You can hate you, and he can hate he"—because Dallon felt the man who would wed his sister had some grain of self-loathing; there had been soul-pain in the future shadow—"but you love each other, you split your souls, I don't know how." Dallon frowned. "But you're going to do the right thing. It feels strange now, but it's right then. You know?"

Dasha dried her eyes and fumbled through his explanation. She shook her head sadly.

"When you do the Dance of the Lady, how do you feel?" Dallon pressed.

"Foolish," Dasha admitted, "and clumsy. I can't see how it would ever please anyone, I look like a peagoose with a sore ankle!"

"But when you're older," Dallon said, "when you have a mate that you've bonded with—knowingly—won't it feel better?"

"I hope!" Dasha almost smiled. "If not I doubt I'll keep him." Now she did smile.

Dallon sat at her feet and smiled, although his head was beginning to ache and the memory of the place fading. "I feel the same when I do the Dance of Men. I keep wanting to giggle, it seems like such nonsense."

He frowned as a bout of prescience attacked him without call. "Your Dance will be very intricate, very… sweeping?" He paused and mouthed the word; what he wanted he couldn't describe. "Your Dance won't be in a circle Dasha, he'll hunt you like the wolf calls to his bride. That's why it all happens, because you don't keep it in the circle." He paused again and the attacking thoughts fled. "I have no idea what I mean." He smiled up at her. "Sorry."

Dasha smiled down and handed him a finished quilt. "That's all right, I never know half of what I mean. Sometimes I think I'm crazy as Mad Maude down the way; she rambles almost as much as I do, but no one listens to her."

"That's because Mad Maude *is* really mad, her mind wandered after that horse kicked her, that's what the healer said. And we have to be respectful because she might be trapped inside, listening, but she can't say what she means." Dallon fully sympathized with Mad Maude. Sharing half a talent with his twin was enough to make anyone crazy.

He fervently wished her the best of luck with a husband, but secretly it didn't surprise him that none of the village lads would have her to wife. He suspected a Lord from a neighboring town might try and claim her, but he didn't know of anyone strong enough to bind her. Magic rolled off his sister, and him, like water off the ducks in the pond.

When Dasha had broken her arm climbing on the roof to race him when they were seven, no healing spell could fix it; they'd had to wait weeks and weeks for the arm to heal itself.

He'd been careful since then not to break anything that would want a healer; Dasha had been miserable.

And as she grew she grew stronger, and only her own magic seemed to affect her.

Maybe, sometimes, he thought a little of his crept in, but certainly no one he knew of was strong enough to catch her. That's what the dance of Men was, a pretty spell to trap women into loving you so they never left your…

"Thoughtless, careless butt?" Dasha finished easily for him.

He shrugged. The mind reading was a remnant of the sharing, it would pass with the growing headache.

"You should go lie down and get some rest before it gets worse," she ordered him warmly.

Dallon stood, smiling. He bobbed his head and exited with the blanket. At the gate he paused to look back. He looked down at the tiny blanket and a chill of dread filled him. "Why won't you talk to her?"

"Because she doesn't need to know the future," Dasha said primly as she picked up a new piece of cloth. "And it's better, for now, if she doesn't know what's going to happen."

Dallon could just imagine the horrors waiting a new mother. The trauma of birth, a blue, frozen child who never breathed, and babe dead in its crib come morning, or the youngster wandered off and lost to the forest or river.

He bit his lip to keep tears from spilling; his head ached fiercely and he didn't want to Know what would happen. "Will she be okay?" he asked softly, praying the mothers' pain would be brief. She wasn't much older than the twins, newly married, nervous, and so happy.

Dasha sighed and drew his attention away from the blanket. "Why is it boys always imagine the terrible fates? There are worse things for a young mother to know than that her babe will die in bearing."

"I can't imagine what," Dallon said.

"For a young mother? Try this: Her husband hasn't even finished their one room cot, and tomorrow, she'll bear twin boys, twin boys as big and strong and handsome and fierce as their father. Just imagine the trouble they'll cause, just imagine the chaos twins of hers will be! And just wait until they're old enough to Dance! She'll have over forty grandchildren from those two alone!" Dasha exclaimed. "Right now she's imagining the sweet little girl with her father's fair curls. She's imagining teaching her daughter the steps to the Dance that won her love. Do you want me to kill those dreams?"

Dallon looked down at the white blanket trimmed in blue, then up at Dasha, who was trimming an identical blanket. "Does she have a girl?" he asked.

"Several, and they're all trouble, I can tell you!" Dasha sounded like Grandmere for a moment. "Give her that blanket, it will turn her thoughts to boys before tomorrow, and lessen the shock. I'll give her this blanket after the birth."

Dallon nodded and walked away. Moments later, stopped, pivoted, and stuck his head back around the corner to the garden. "*Forty*? Are you sure?"

"The family tends to multiples at births. Twins and triplets will be their norm. But no fears, all the babes live, and if they make good choices they'll be long and happy lives."

Dallon left shaking his aching head and making note not to marry into either family. He'd had his fill of twins for a lifetime.

THE MAKING OF *DANCER, DREAMER, SEER*

This originally started as the prologue to a story. I could picture Dasha on a battlefield across from someone who had half her soul… But that's as far as I ever got. I knew the image and emotion. If I had some art skill maybe I could have drawn it or painted it. But I was never particularly good with drawing, and I haven't developed the patience physical art needs, so I stuck to writing.

Echoes of this story can be seen in others of my books. Sometimes that's how it goes: not every good idea gets to be a full book, and that's okay. Maybe someone else will write an ending for Dallon and Dasha.

Read more by Liana Brooks!

FLEET OF MALIK: BODIES IN MOTION
CHAPTER ONE

THE PROBLEM WITH VACATIONS, Selena reflected as she adjusted her sweater outside Cargo Blue, was that reality was always waiting at the end. A quick search of the local security cameras found one that showed the peeling sunburn on her right shoulder blade.

Such was the curse of pale-skinned, ship-born Fleet personnel. Anytime she left the foggy belts covering the city of Tarrin, she barbecued like a shrimp, no matter how much sunscreen she applied. Otherwise, she'd flee even further from the Fleet Enclave and make her home on the equatorial beaches of the planet they were trapped on.

She panned the camera and checked her left shoulder. Black ink made a starscape that disguised three silver scars as shooting stars. The painting covered her shoulder blade and part of her upper arm. As the artist had promised, the skin-paint had kept her from burning as much, though it still had the over-stretched feel of a burn. With a few adjustments, her uniform covered most of the temporary art; it would keep her from having to explain to her colleagues.

Her forearm warmed, a warning that someone was about to contact her through the tech implant tucked between her radius and ulna.

She hesitated too long and the call came through, a persistent ping against her skull as the phantom image of her best friend floated on the edge of her vision.

Selena turned off the visual receiver and answered. "Genevieve," she said with a smile as the image of her vivacious, red-headed friend appeared floating against the backdrop of landing gear that supported the grounded fleet.

A grounder would have thought she was talking to herself, but grounders wouldn't set foot near the neo-city-state of

Enclave. The rocky beach served as a city and tomb for the survivors of the last war.

"Selena!" Gen gushed. "Starcom to Selena. Where are you? I'm covering for now."

"Delayed, but almost there." Selena hoped Gen wouldn't hear the lie. She'd been standing in the shadows of the Enclave pub for nearly a quarter hour.

"The *Lorenza* could get here faster," Gen said, referencing a long-dead ship whose crew were found skeletonized at their stations. Gen blew hair off her face. "Stars above, you're an hour late. The whole fleet is flying faster than you."

Selena turned on her visual long enough to roll her eyes at her friend. "Ha, ha, funny. That joke needs to be forcibly retired." Sooner rather than later. The fleet couldn't fly without fuel, and the Malik system they were stranded in held precious few deposits of the orun crystals needed to power the ships.

"If you don't come," Gen said threateningly, "I will teleport to your apartment and drag you out in your pajamas."

"I'm not at home," Selena admitted. And she wouldn't have let her best friend come to her new house if she was.

Gen was smart enough to realize that the small palace Selena had bought in downtown Tarrin wasn't paid for by her official OIA salary. The paygrades for the Office of Imperial Affairs had last been updated when the Malik system was still in contact with the empire, making them 900 years out of date.

Technically, taking a second job wasn't treason, but there were enough people in the fleet who'd see it as a betrayal that keeping it secret felt right. Especially since Gen's captain was one who would scream the loudest.

Gen clapped. "Selena! Stop stalling yer engines and get in here. This isn't some Fleet Tribunal, just our friends. You, me, Carver. I left a message for Marshall. You know. People we like."

The light of understanding dawned. "Carver? This is so you can snuggle up to Perrin Carver without your parents watching?"

"Yes," Gen admitted, not looking the least bit contrite.

"You're only dragging me along so I can cover for you while you make out in a corner, aren't you?" She masked the relief with mock anger. At least Gen wasn't trying to set Selena up with one of her cousins. Or, ancestors forbid, Gen's handsy older brother.

Again.

Gen opened her eyes wide with an innocent smile. "Maybe."

"Gen!" Selena rolled her eyes. "Doesn't he have his own place?"

"Just the bachelor's dorm. The Carvers didn't have any ships except the shuttle his parents crashed in. Making out next door to Mom and Dad? No. And the BOQ? It's so tacky. You can hear everything through those walls."

Selena hid a smile. "I'll be there soon enough."

If Gen ever caught wind of how panicky the thought of a relationship made her, Gen would make it her life's goal to see Selena paired off. And there wasn't a man alive who she could imagine getting close to now.

Her implant helpfully pulled up an image of a tall, broad-shouldered, lean-muscled fighter with skin black as the night between stars and emerald-green eyes.

She pushed the memory away.

Lieutenant Commander Titan Sciarra was striking, intelligent, and had a body she'd cross battle lines for, but he was also out of reach. There was no point in chasing a man who wouldn't give her the time of day.

Another crew shuffled past her into the bar, black patches with silver fists on their shoulders.

It was getting harder to pretend she belonged in Enclave, with the fleet. Once upon a time, she'd known every crew's patch without thinking. She could name captains, their ships and their seconds by rote.

Now she would need to tap into the fleet's information nexus if she wanted to know who they were.

She stopped at the edge of the door to tug her lightest shields into place. A few minor adjustments would keep bugs away, keep beer off her clothes, and prevent anyone from hacking into her implant. They could still send messages, because disallowing that would have raised eyebrows. And they could still hit her. But she could always hit back.

Selena rolled her shoulders and strutted into Cargo Blue. It was a battle-field, but she was the last captain of the Caryll family, and she wasn't going down without a fight.

Whatever crew owned Cargo Blue probably hadn't had much of a decorating budget, but at least they'd stuck with a theme: oversized cargo boxes were piled up to make walls, seating, and tables. Olive-green safety webbing draped from the ceiling between blue lights. Fog used for fire drills on the ships pumped across the floor to hide the concrete beneath.

There was no bouncer at the door, but people were still hanging around the entrance.

As a rule, the fleet was cautious, and the young faces she saw belonged to fleet members who had never ventured outside their own crew more than a few times, even though the fleet had been grounded for nearly three years.

Tables to the left, bar ahead, dance floor to the right… and that meant the back half of the cargo hanger had been partitioned and karaoke would be in the back right corner. After a few minutes of weaving through the human crush, she found Gen, already sitting in Perrin Carver's lap and giggling.

"Selena!" Gen jumped up and hugged her. "I was beginning to worry!"

"How many people are in here?" Selena shouted over the music.

"Everyone under forty?" Gen laughed. With a small hand wave Gen put up a minor sound shield, muting the music. "People are going to stir crazy. Combine that with the anniversary—"

The anniversary.

Today.

The day the war had begun, the day the united fleet had died.

They'd been dying for four hundred years, well aware that the reserve of orun crystals was depleted and there was no way to move forward with the ships they had.

Old Captain Baular had seen the deposit of orun on the fifth planet as their saving grace. He'd get it even if it meant killing the grounders.

And, coward that he was, he'd ordered his grandson to lead the first attack instead of leading it himself.

That opening skirmish began and ended in the dark, with Titan Sciarra in the infirmary, and five Academy fighters mis-sing or damaged. But by lunch of the next day, every officer belonging to crews allied with the Baulars withdrew.

Seven months later, heated words turned to live rounds.

"Selena?" Gen asked quietly, placing a hand on her arm. "You didn't know the date, did you?"

"I was trying not to think about." If she had, she'd have cut her vacation to the islands early. Maybe even made her pilgrimage to the small cay where she'd ditched her stolen fighter after driving off the attack.

She rolled her shoulder, stretching the deep scars. "It snuck up on me."

"First round, we drink to the Lost Fleet, and all who've gone on to crew it. I'm buying," Gen said with a touch of forced joviality. "Carver's been making friends. Tell her, babe." She pushed Carver's shoulder.

Perrin Carver was tall, broad-shouldered man with shy, hazel eyes that hid a wicked sense of humor.

Selena's heart fluttered just a little at the memory of a time when she'd fancied herself in love with him. He'd been the ideal starsider: intelligent, good-looking, and charismatic. They'd been friends of a sort, but even that relationship had soured when she'd realized he'd been getting close to her so he could learn more about Genevieve Silar.

Carver nodded and held out his hand. "Hi, Selena. How are you?"

She tapped the back of his hand with hers, letting him test her shields. "Good. How's the Starguard?"

"Booming." The Starguard's commander smiled, white teeth flashing, but there was a tightness around his eyes. "Everyone hears about guardians being allowed outside the Enclave, or working with the Jhandarmi, and I'm drowning in recruiting requests. Captains of larger crews invite me to Captain's Mess so they can introduce me to their best and brightest. Half the time I can't tell if they want me to marry into the crew or take the fleetlings into the guard." His shield was still attached to hers, scanning her as he talked.

All he would get from her was polite interest. Her heartrate didn't spike or dip at the mention of the Jhandarmi. Her smile never flickered.

"Maybe you should lock down Gen," Selena said. "If you had a spouse, no one would try to get you to marry into the crew."

Carver and Gen shared a look, and Gen sent a ping of information that Selena's implant translated as an ongoing debate over crew name and a place to live.

Carver sent something similar; a picture of his bachelor's quarters and his one ship.

There was no room for them to marry and have a family.

"Enclave is a temporary solution," Selena said out loud. She'd lost the taste for communicating by implant years ago. "If we—"

A heavy hand wrapped around her waist as someone wearing too much cologne stepped far too close to her. "Hello, Selena."

Hollis Silar, one of Gen's many siblings, kissed her temple.

Simultaneously, Selena sighed, sent a shock through her shield to Hollis's hand, and elbowed him in the gut. "Hi, Hollis. I see you're still bathing in cologne rather than water."

He stepped away from her, an easy smile still in place.

It wasn't that Hollis was bad looking; plenty of women found him handsome.

It was that he was equally affectionate with every woman he saw and he couldn't keep a secret to save his life. Or anyone else's.

He'd chase anyone with a pretty smile and fell in and out of love a couple of times a day.

"Nice to see you too, Selena. Now, everyone, you're all going to look at me, smile, and laugh like I'm my normal, dashing self," he said, his smile never changing. "You haven't been paying attention, but I'm not a member of the Starguard for nothing. We're being watched. Now take your nice drinks from the waitress and keep your eyes on me."

Hollis nodded to the waitress and handed out four cups with bright purple liquid. "Bruised Stars all around. Guaranteed to make you giggle, or so the guy at the bar told me. Although he's a Seutaai, so take it with a shield in place." He handed Selena her drink with a smile, but immediately glanced over his shoulder.

"Big brother, who are we looking for?" Gen asked with a slow drawl. "Is it a friend who you might have forgotten to call back after a night out?"

Hollis shook his head. "No, I thought I saw some of the Lee crew. Make that, I'm certain of it."

Selena grimaced. "As long as Rowena isn't here."

"Did you call me?"

Startled, Selena looked up to the face of her least favorite woman: Rowena Lee.

"Hello," Selena said politely. "I see you're still alive. That's…"

Unfortunate.

She nodded and took a slug of her Bruised Star.

Rowena held up a tray of electric blue shots. "My crew thinks I can't out-drink anyone in this bar. I probably can't go toe-to-toe with alcoholics like the Silars here. But No-Shot Selena?" Rowena set the drinks on the table. "I can out-shoot you in the stars or on the ground."

Gen sucked in air between her teeth and sent Selena several urgent pings telling her to ignore the Lees.

Selena muted Gen. "I took plenty of shots in the war. As I recall, I disabled three of your big birds. *Bassi, Aryton, Theoano*... Bang, bang, bang." Selena mimed firing with her finger. "Three shots. Three silent ships."

"Not kills," Rowena said. "A whole war and you never blooded yourself."

That was it, the memory she didn't want to face; the time she'd almost taken Death's claim and risked killing someone outside of war.

"That's uncalled for," Hollis said, trying to step between them. "Selena, why don't we—"

Selena pushed Hollis aside and grabbed the first shot.

She tossed back the potent drink and shattered the glass on the table. "Go suck vacuum, Rowena. You're a pissant yeoman with no hope of command."

"I went to the Academy, same as you, Selena. I fought for the fleet." Rowena slammed a shot back. "You fought for the mud-lickers."

Selena took another shot as the first started to fuzz her judgement. "I prevented the Baulars from committing mass genocide and destroying the civilians along with the fleet."

Rowena took her second shot. A crowd was gathering and that seemed to feed her cruelty. "The Lees survived the war. We're still here. How many Caryll captains are there? Oh, right, one. Can you count that high, No-Shot? You have any idea how easy it would be for me to end you right now?"

Selena took the last two glasses and slammed them both back.

Gen pinged her, giving locations, counts, and identities of the Lee allies in the crowd.

Hollis stepped to her flank, ready to defend her.

She stood, anger burning through her veins. "Sure, your crew outnumbers mine. I guess on paper, it's not really a fair fight, is it, Rowena? But you were trained as a flight leader, and what do Carylls do? Hand-to-hand combat. Maybe I should

thin your ranks, starting with one mouthy
yeoman.”

Keep reading! Head to:
www.inkprintpress.com/lianabrooks/
malik/bodies/

ABOUT THE AUTHOR

LIANA BROOKS lives a quiet, unassuming life somewhere in the Americas where she is absolutely *not* plotting to take over the world.

When she isn't being perfectly normal and average, Liana enjoys writing science fiction in every form, from sprawling space opera romances (the *Fleet of Malik* series) to the antics of a super-powered family (the *Heroes and Villains* series).

Liana also maintains a soft spot for paranormal romances. She writes the popular *All I Want For Christmas* novellas, including *All I Want For Christmas Is A Werewolf* and *All I Want For Christmas Is A Reaper*.

You can learn more about her and her books at www.LianaBrooks.com.

INKLETS

Collect them all! Released on the 1st and 15th of each month.

INKLET #079
Shadows
NEVER LIE
AMY LAURENS

INKLET #080
Here She Lies
LIANA BROOKS

INKLET #081
Perfect
Destruction
An Age Of Unicorns Story
AMY LAURENS

INKLET #082
What Blood
Can Do
AMY LAURENS

INKLET #083
Dancer, Dreamer
Seer
LIANA BROOKS

INKLET #084
As Time
Whirls Slowly
Past
AMY LAURENS

INKLET #085
Far More
Satisfying
Than Hell
AMY LAURENS

INKLET #086
Just
Another Day
In Hell
LIANA BROOKS

INKLET #087
Moon AND
Morning
AMY LAURENS

INKLET #098
Some
Impropriety
Expected
AMY LAURENS

INKLET #089
NEON SNOW
LIANA BROOKS

INKLET #090
Reincarnation
LIANA BROOKS

INKLET #091
More Than
Mushrooms
AMY LAURENS

DOUBLE ISSUE
INKLET #092
How To Make A Star
& The World Ended
LIANA BROOKS

INKLET #093
CAUGHT
IN THE ACT
AMY LAURENS

INKLET #094
ANUBIS
Has Sent You
Six Souls
LIANA BROOKS

INKLET #095
PRAYER TO A
GODDESS
LIANA BROOKS

INKLET #096
Love In The
Time Of Corona
AMY LAURENS